THE GREAT
TALKING
CONTEST

GEORGE SHEA

For Anique and all good birds around the world
Illustrations by Lane Yerkes

Copyright © 1989, 1978 by George Shea.
All rights reserved. Published by Scholastic Inc.
SPRINT and SPRINT BOOKS are trademarks of Scholastic Inc.
Printed in the U.S.A.
ISBN 0-590-35183-4

5 6 7 8 9 10   31   03 02 01 00 99 98

CHAPTER 1

The whole crazy thing began that Saturday afternoon. We were playing softball, and we were behind 9-8. I was pitching. It wasn't a big game, but it was a close one. My name is Lorna — Lorna Lang.

Scott Melfi was up. The bases were loaded. "Come on, Lorna! Strike me out!" he yelled. "Come on! You can do it! You can do it!" He was waving the bat around in the air. Scott is a real clown.

I started to throw a pitch. Just then I heard: "AWWKKK!! AWWKKK!! AWWKKK!!" The sounds were coming from the bushes behind home plate.

I stopped. "What was that?" I asked.

"It's a bird," said Mark Halsey, the catcher. "Come on. Let's play ball!"

I started to throw again.

"AWWKKK!! AWWKKK!! AWWKKK!!" came the sounds again. It sounded as if something was in trouble.

"Hold it," I said. I ran off the mound. There was something on the ground near the bushes. It was a large, brightly colored bird. It was a parrot — mostly green and yellow, with a thick, curved beak. A lot of its feathers were scattered on the ground.

A large dog stood near it. The dog was trying to pick it up in its mouth. The bird went for the dog with its beak. It missed. The bird's wings were flapping around, but the bird couldn't fly. Something was wrong with it.

The dog went for it again with its teeth.

"NO!" I yelled. I tried to shoo the dog away. "Get away! Get away!" I yelled. I stood between the dog and the bird. The bird was making noises again. I couldn't believe what I heard. The bird seemed to be saying: "HELP ME! AWWK! HELP ME! AWWK! AWWK!"

I thought about picking it up. Maybe it would bite me, but I didn't care. I picked it up. Scott and Janie came running up.

"What is it, Lorna?" Scott asked.

Just then the dog leaped up at me. It went straight for the parrot. I held it away — as high as I could. Scott was holding a baseball bat in his hand.

"Keep that dog away!" I yelled. Scott and Janie stood between me and the dog.

I walked back to the ball field with the parrot. All the other kids came running over.

"What is it?" Janie asked.

"It's a parrot," I said.

Suddenly the parrot whistled. "Whoo-hoo!

Whoo-hoo! Oh, boy!" it said.

"It talks!" Janie said.

"Of course it talks," I said. "It's a parrot! A lot of parrots can talk."

"Wow!" Janie said. "What's your name, fella?" she asked. "How much is two and two?"

"Whoo-hoo! Oh, boy! Oh, boy!" the parrot said again.

"It doesn't answer questions," I said. "It can't *think* the way we can."

"I heard it say 'Help me! Help me!'" said Janie. "How come it said that if it can't think?"

"I guess somebody taught it to say that when it was in trouble," I said. "Anyway, the poor thing's hurt."

Suddenly the bird looked up again. It looked me right in the eye.

"You're pretty! You're pretty!" it said.

"Hey," I said. "It thinks I'm pretty!"

"Maybe it can talk," said Scott. "But it's sure not very smart." Some of the kids laughed.

"Listen," I said. "I've got to take this bird to some place where it'll be safe."

"But what about the game?" Scott asked. "We need you to pitch."

"Let's finish the game first," said Mark.

"But maybe it'll die," I said.

"Why don't you take it home, Lorna?" Janie said. "Come on, I'll go with you."

CHAPTER 2

Janie and I left the ball field. Scott was mad. "How are we going to play with five on a side?" he yelled after us. Right then I didn't care about the game very much. I only cared about getting the parrot to my house.

I carried the parrot in both hands. I didn't know if this was a good idea. I was afraid I would drop it. I was afraid it would start jumping around. But it didn't. It lay very still in my hands. Maybe it understood that I wanted to help it. Or maybe it was just too weak and hurt to do anything. It didn't say a word all the way home. But as soon as we got there, it started to talk.

"Whoo-hoo! Oh, boy! Oh, boy! *Bonne chance!* Hey, Cookie! *Auf wiedersehen,* Charlie! *Bueno! Bueno!*"

"What's it saying?" asked Janie.

"I don't know. But it doesn't sound like English," I said.

There was no one home. We took the parrot upstairs to my room. Janie spread some newspapers out on the floor, and I set the bird on top of them.

"Let's get it some water," I said.

"How about some food?" said Janie. "What do parrots eat?"

We went downstairs to the kitchen. We filled a small bowl with water. I found some whole-wheat bread. I broke it up into little pieces and I put them on a plate. Then back up we went. I set the water and the bread down in front of the parrot.

It didn't take a bite. It wasn't moving. It wasn't moving at all. Its eyes were shut. I got scared.

"Maybe it's — ," Janie said.

"Maybe it's just asleep," I said.

Janie poked it with her finger. It didn't move. She poked it again. It moved one of its legs just a little — and very slowly.

"Now I'm scared," said Janie.

"So am I," I said. "It looks really — "

Just then there was a noise downstairs. My mother was home. My mother wasn't crazy about having strange animals in the house. But I had to tell her sooner or later. I went downstairs.

"Mom," I began. "Janie and I found a parrot in the park. It talks."

"That's nice," said my mother. She was busy putting away groceries. I didn't think she really heard me.

"It got hurt by a dog. I brought it home."

She heard that. "You brought it home!" she said. "Lorna, I told you not to bring home any more animals."

"But it was so helpless," I said. "Somebody

13

had to help it."

"I don't care," she said. "I told you . . . "
Then she stopped. "A parrot?" she said. "Did you say a parrot? What was a parrot doing in the park?"

"I don't know," I answered.

"It speaks a lot of different languages," Janie piped up.

"A bird like that must belong to somebody," said my mother. Then she got this look on her face. She started shaking her head from side to side. My mother is really OK, but she's not too crazy about stray animals. She's really not.

I am. I bring them home all the time. If I found a sick worm, I'd bring it home. As a matter of fact, I think I *did* once.

"Lorna — " she began.

"I think it might die," I said.

"I just wish you'd stop bringing home all these sick animals," she said. "Last week you brought home that frog. The week before, you brought home that cat."

The cat. "Oh, my gosh, THE CAT!!" I said. I'd forgotten all about the cat. It was in the house. I heard it yowling upstairs. I'd left the door to my room open. The sound was coming from my room.

I ran for the stairs. Janie was right behind me. I hoped we weren't too late.

15

CHAPTER 3

I was afraid we were too late. I could hear the parrot.

"AWWKKK! AWWKKK!! OH, BOY! OH, BOY! HELP ME! HELP ME!" the parrot screamed. It was still on the newspaper. It was on its back, but it was trying to get up. The cat was almost on top of it. The cat had its back up in the air. Its tail stood straight up too.

It hissed and poked at the parrot's body with its sharp claws. There were little specks of blood all over the paper. I ran at the cat and drove it back against the far wall.

"Get the parrot, Janie!" I said. "Get it out of here!"

I reached for a chair. I hoped I could hold the cat back with the chair. I felt like a lion tamer in the circus.

Janie picked up the parrot and started for the door. I backed the cat up into a corner. It hissed and swung its claws at the chair. Janie went out the door. I threw down the chair in the cat's way. Then I ran out the door and closed it just in time.

We took the bird downstairs. Janie put it down on the kitchen floor.

"Gosh," she said. "That cat really wanted to kill it!"

I could see flecks of blood on its feathers. Upstairs the cat was still yowling.

"Lorna, this is crazy," my mother said. "You've got to stop bringing all these sick animals home."

"I *know*, Mom," I said. "But what are we going to do? It might die!"

"Lorna!" she answered. I could see she was angry. She looked away.

I waited a minute or two. Then I said: "Why don't we take it to Doc Sykes?" Doc Sykes was a veterinarian. He had a pet hospital in town.

"I don't know," she said. "That could cost a lot of money."

"Please, Mom," I said. "It'll die. I know it will! Just look at it!"

She looked down at the bird. It looked back up at her. "You're . . . pretty. . . . You're . . . pretty," it croaked.

My mother looked as if she was going to cry. I guess she was beginning to feel sorry for it. "All right," she said finally. "We'll take it to Doc Sykes."

We drove to Doc Sykes' pet hospital. Doc was really surprised when he saw the parrot. "Lorna," he said, "I didn't know you had a parrot!"

"I don't," I said. "We found it in the park. A dog was — "

"It looks terrible," he said. He took out a stethoscope. He placed it on the bird's chest. He used it to listen to its breathing. Doc looked very unhappy. "It's got pneumonia," he finally said. "It's very serious. It's like a very, very bad cold. These birds get colds very easily. That's why you've got to keep them warm."

"Doc, could — could it die?" Janie asked.

"Yes, it could," he said. "Also, it's a little banged up. What happened to it?"

"A dog went after it in the park," I said. "Then my cat — "

"Well, they didn't hurt it badly," he said. "These wounds will heal. The real problem is the pneumonia."

He squeezed a tube of white medicine onto the wounds. "Now I'm going to give it a shot for the pneumonia," he said. He filled a needle with another medicine. I held the bird still. He stuck the needle into its chest. The bird let out a big "AWWWK!!" Then it was quiet again.

"That's all I can do right now," said Doc Sykes. "It must have already been sick when the dog got to it. Parrots usually put up a good fight. A big parrot can beat a dog or even a cat in a fight. They have big beaks and they can do a lot of damage with them."

Doc picked up a handful of seeds. He held them up to the bird's beak. "Here now, birdie," he said. "Time to eat."

"Eat . . . eat," it croaked. It picked up a few seeds with its beak. But its eyes were only half-open.

"It's a Yellow-Necked Amazon," said Doc. "That's what they call this kind of parrot. They're South American birds. They're terrific talkers. They like people too."

"Can — can I take it home with me?" I asked.

"No," said Doc. "I had better keep it here. If it lives through tonight, it should be all right. You go home now," he said. "I'll call you in the morning."

Mom and I dropped Janie off at her house. Then we went home.

I didn't sleep much that night.

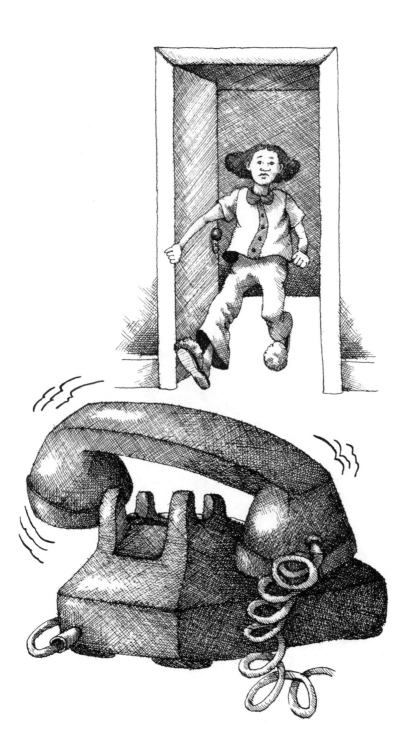

CHAPTER 4

The next morning, bright and early, the phone rang. I jumped out of bed and ran to answer it.

"Hello?" I said.

"Good morning!" said a voice on the other end.

"Good morning," I said. "Who is this?"

"Good morning!" the voice said again. It wasn't anyone I knew.

"Good morning!" I said. "Who is this?"

"Good morning," said the voice again.

Now I was getting annoyed. "Who *are* you?" I asked.

"I'm Annie! I'm Annie! Whoo-hoo! Who-hoo! Oh, boy!" said the voice. Then I knew. It was the parrot's voice! Doc got on the phone.

"How do you like Annie?" he asked. I could hear her going "Awwk! Awwk!" as Doc spoke.

"I like her a lot," I said. "So she's a girl, huh?"

"She says she is," said Doc. "She's going to be all right. I had better keep her a few more days. But she'll be fine. There's only one problem now."

"What's that?" I asked.

23

"Finding out who owns her," Doc said. "How would you like to go on television?"

"Television!" I said. "Sure!"

"It would be a good way to find Annie's owner," Doc said. "I have a friend who works for Channel 10 News."

A few days later, there we were — on television. Janie, Annie, and I were in Doc's hospital. Annie was perched on my shoulder. A

TV camera was in front of us. A reporter named Sue McCall stood next to us. She held a mike in her hand. She was going to ask us questions.

I was really nervous. I'd never been on TV before.

"Where did you find Annie?" she asked me.

"I found her in Deering Park," I said.

Janie piped up: "Lorna saved her from a dog."

"Well, that makes you a bit of a heroine," said Sue McCall.

"I — I guess so," I answered. I still felt pretty nervous.

"And you don't know who the parrot belongs to?" she asked.

"No," I said. "I'd like to keep her. But I'm sure the owner wants her back."

"Maybe Annie can tell us something," said Sue McCall. "Who feeds you, Annie?" she asked.

"Doc!" said Annie. "Hey, Doc! Hey, Doc! Whoo-hoo! Oh, boy!"

Doc Sykes came over and smiled for the TV camera.

Sue McCall turned and looked at the camera. "We'd like to find out who owns Annie," she said. "If Annie is your bird, please call Dr. Sykes' pet hospital. Call tonight after eight o'clock. This is Sue McCall for Channel 10 News."

And that was it. It was over. Our part of the show was on tape. A few hours later we watched ourselves on television. Then we sat at Doc's and waited for the phone to ring.

Maybe this sounds awful, but I was almost hoping that no one would call. If no one did, then maybe I could keep Annie. I really felt bad about giving her up.

Soon it was eight o'clock, and the phone rang. I picked it up.

"Hello?" I said.

"Hello. This is Sir Wembley Weems," said a voice. "I just saw my dear Annie on television."

"Oh, is Annie your bird?" I said.

"Yes, she is. I'm so happy she's alive and well. I was so worried! I've been looking all over for her. I'd like to come over to pick up the poor dear and take her home."

"Well, sure," I said. I felt bad about letting Annie go. I turned to Annie.

"Annie — it's Mr. Weems," I said. "He's coming to take you home!"

Annie didn't say anything. She just looked away. Then she put her head under one wing.

"You know, you really should get a reward," Mr. Weems said, "for saving Annie."

"Oh, I don't know," I said. "I just — "

26

"I'll be right over," he said. He hung up.

"Who was that?" asked Doc.

"A man named Wembley Weems," I said.

"*Wembley Weems!*" said Doc. "He's one of the richest men in the world. So Annie is *his* parrot!"

A few minutes later the phone rang again.

"Hello," said another voice. "This is Captain Jack Faraday. I want to thank you for taking care of my Annie. Put her on the phone. I want to talk to her."

Now I didn't know what to do. Did Annie have another owner? Which one was the *real* owner?

CHAPTER 5

"Hey, Annie! Hey, Annie!" called out the voice on the phone.

I put Annie next to the phone.

"Hey, Annie!" called out the voice. "It's Jack!"

"Hey, Jack! Hey, Jack!" answered Annie. She looked very excited. Her head was bobbing up and down. She was hopping around on both feet.

"How are you, girl? How are you doing?"

"Fine, Jack! Oh, boy!" said Annie.

"Jack loves Annie!" said the man named Jack.

"Annie loves Jack!" said Annie. "Oh, yes! Awk! Awk! For sure! Awk! Awk!"

"Hey, let me talk to Lorna!" said Jack.

I got back on the phone.

"Lorna, you've just made an old sea dog very happy," said Jack. "That's what I am. An old sea dog! Now listen. I'm over here at the Old Sailors' Hospital. Could you bring Annie over here right away?"

I didn't know what to say. "Well . . . I . . . sure . . . I guess. . . ."

"That's great!" he said. He hung up.

"Wait!" I said. But it was too late.

I turned to Doc and Janie. "What do we do now?" I asked. "Who's the real owner?"

"I think that's easy to see," said Doc. "He's the second one who called. Annie talked her head off to him."

"She didn't talk to the other one at all," said Janie.

Doc told us to take Annie over to the Old Sailors' Hospital. He said he'd take care of

Wembley Weems when he showed up.

Janie and I took off for the hospital. We carried Annie in a big cage that had a cover over it.

The Old Sailors' Hospital was really an interesting place. It looked like a ship. All the windows looked like portholes. There were pictures and models of ships all over the place.

A man stopped us at the door.

"I'm sorry," he said. "But you can't bring that in here."

"We can't bring what in here?" I said. "This isn't Godzilla. It's just a parrot! See?" I took the cover off the cage. There was Annie. She looked the man right in the eye.

"You're pretty! You're pretty!" she said.

"She's funny, huh?" said Janie.

The man didn't even smile. "*I* don't think it's so funny," he said. "Anyway, it can't go into any of the rooms where there are sick people."

"All right," I said. I asked Janie to wait in the lobby with Annie. I went upstairs to see Captain Jack.

Captain Jack was an old, old man with a long white beard. He was wearing a bathrobe and sitting up in a chair. The first thing he said was: "Hey, where's Annie?"

"I'm Lorna," I said.

"I know you're Lorna!" he said. "I saw you on

TV. But where's Annie?"

"They wouldn't let her upstairs," I said.

"They can't do that!" he said. "Not *now*! I got this big chocolate fudge cake and her favorite blanket and everything!"

I saw a big chocolate fudge cake on the table beside his bed. There was a little gray blanket there too. It had a little "A" sewn on it.

"I was going to have a little party for her," he said.

Just then the phone beside Jack's bed rang. He answered it.

"It's for you," he said.

It was Janie. "Lorna! ANNIE'S LOOSE! SHE'S GONE! SHE'S — "

"I'll be right down!" I said.

I headed out of the room. "My friend just lost something," I yelled to Captain Jack. "I'll be right back!"

I got downstairs. I couldn't believe what I saw. A bunch of doctors and nurses and guards were chasing Annie all around the lobby.

"AWWK! AWWK!" screamed Annie. "Kiss me! Kiss me!"

The front door opened. Annie flew out. Janie and I ran outside. It was getting dark and we couldn't see her.

"Listen," I said to Janie. "Just *listen*! Maybe we can *hear* her."

CHAPTER 6

We listened. After a minute we heard: "Whoo-hoo! Oh, boy! Oh, boy!" Annie was out there somewhere.

There were a lot of trees around the hospital. "I'll bet she's up in the trees," I said. I headed back upstairs.

I ran into Jack's room. "Annie's loose!" I said. I pointed to the window. "I think she's out there — in one of the trees!"

Captain Jack opened the window. "Annie!" he called. "Hey, Annie! It's Jack!"

"Hey, Jack! Hey, Jack!" we could hear Annie call from the trees. But we still couldn't see her.

Then she came flying in the window. She landed right on Jack's shoulder. "Hey, girl!" Jack shouted. He kissed her right on the beak.

"Quick, Lorna, shut the door!" Jack said. "I don't want the nurses to hear her."

I went and shut the door. Jack gave Annie a piece of chocolate fudge cake. "Hey! My kind of cake! My kind of cake!" Annie said. Then she and Jack started talking to each other. They did a little act together.

"How's my Annie?" asked Jack.

"I'm pretty! Whoo-hoo! I'm pretty!" she answered.

"Yes, you are!" Jack said. "How much is two and two?"

"Five!" Annie crowed happily.

"No, it's not!" said Jack. "It's only *four*."

"It's only *for* what?" squawked Annie.

Jack was laughing. We were all laughing. "No, it's *four*!" he said.

Just then the phone rang again. Annie went over and knocked it off the hook with her beak. Jack laughed. "Who's it *for*, Annie?" he asked.

"For you!" she said. Jack laughed again.

But it wasn't for Jack. It was for me.

It was Doc.

"Wembley Weems just left," he said. "He was very angry because Annie wasn't here. He said he'll give you five thousand dollars to return Annie to him."

"Five thousand dollars!" I said. "But Annie isn't his. Can Weems prove that he owns her?"

"No, he can't," said Doc. "I just thought I'd better warn you. He told me he'd do anything to get her back."

"WEEMS!" Jack shot up suddenly. "THAT CROOK! He's been after my Annie for years!"

"I'll talk to you later, Doc," I said.

"Why does Weems want Annie?" I asked Captain Jack.

"Because of the contest," said Jack.

"What contest?" I asked.

"The World's-Record Talking Parrot Contest," said Jack. "It's a contest to find the best talking parrot in the world. It's being held soon in this city. And Annie is going to win."

"Annie's the best talking parrot in the *whole world*?" asked Janie.

"She sure is," said Jack. "Annie loves to talk. She knows over 250 words. She can speak 14 different languages. She can say all the words in *Rudolph, the Red-Nosed Reindeer.*"

"Wow!" Janie and I said together.

"She's going to win," said Jack. "And Wembley is unhappy about it. Wembley owns the second-best talking parrot in the world. But second place isn't good enough for him. He hates to lose.

"Wembley's been after me for years to sell Annie to him. But I've always said no. I've had Annie for 40 years. We love each other. We've sailed on ships all over the world together."

"Fifteen men on a dead man's chest!" piped up Annie.

"How did she get lost?" Janie asked.

"I got sick," said Jack. "I had to go into this hospital. I left her with a friend. I guess old Annie missed me. She flew away to find me. That's when she got sick and you found her."

After a while a nurse walked in. When she saw Annie, she told us we had to leave.

Jack put Annie back in her cage. He put the little gray blanket in the cage with her. "She sleeps with it every night," he said. "She wraps it around her with her beak. And this is a record Annie likes to listen to."

I took the record and we left. We took the bus home. It was late when we got there. It was a little scary too. All the way home I had the feeling we were being watched.

We got near my house. A big car was parked outside. Its lights were on. The lights went off as soon as we got close.

"I'm scared. I don't like this," I said to Janie.

CHAPTER 7

"Quick! Let's go around the back way," I said to Janie.

We cut across the front lawn of the house next door.

"Awwk! Awwk! What's the hurry? What's the hurry?" Annie screamed.

We made it to the back door of my house. We got in. I looked out the front window. But the car was gone.

I kept a lookout for the car for the next few days. But I didn't see it again. I kept Annie at my house. She watched a lot of TV.

Then Jack called. "I'm getting out of the hospital today," he said. "Just in time, too! Today's the day of the contest!"

"I'll have Annie waiting for you," I said. "She's all ready for the contest."

She was ready, all right. She had been talking her head off. I had played the record Jack had given me over and over again for Annie. It had a lot of words on it, and Annie repeated all of them.

That afternoon I started off early to meet Jack. I took Annie through the park, which was on our way. It was a nice day, and I thought she would

like some fresh air and sunshine.

I sat down on a bench. Her cage was next to me.

An old woman came along and sat down on the next bench. When she saw Annie, she came over. "What a nice parrot!" she said. "Do you think she'd like some toasted bread crumbs?"

"Why don't you put a few in her cage?" I said. "Maybe she'll eat them."

The woman put some bread crumbs in the cage. Annie started to peck at them.

A hungry squirrel came over. It was up on its
hind legs, begging for food.

"Here," the woman said. "Why don't you give
that squirrel some bread crumbs?"

I got up to feed the squirrel. I threw it a few
crumbs.

In a flash the woman grabbed Annie's cage
and took off, running.

"HELP ME!" Annie screamed. "AWWK!! AWKK!
HELP ME!!"

I ran after the woman. She ran awfully fast

43

for a person that old. I couldn't believe how fast she was.

I chased her to the edge of the park. "STOP HER!" I shouted. "SHE'S GOT MY PARROT!"

A big white car was waiting at the edge of the park. She jumped in, and the car took off. I ran after it. I wanted to get the license number, but there wasn't any license plate. It was the same car that had been outside my house.

"Weems!" I thought to myself. "That was no gray-haired lady! That was Weems!"

I called the police. Then I walked back through the park. I felt awful. What would

Weems do to Annie? How could I tell Jack that I had let Annie be kidnapped?

I walked back to the same park bench. Beside the bench was the squirrel I'd been feeding. It lay on the ground. It wasn't moving. I knelt down beside it. I couldn't believe it. There must have been something in the bread crumbs!

After a few minutes the police came along. I told them what had happened. I showed them the squirrel and the bread crumbs. They took a few of the crumbs as evidence.

I felt sorry for the squirrel. I didn't want to leave it there on the ground. A dog or cat might get to it.

"You want a ride somewhere?" one of the police officers asked me.

"OK," I said. I picked up the squirrel and a few bread crumbs. I asked the police to take me to Doc Sykes' place.

They drove me to Doc's. Doc looked the squirrel over. "It's alive," he said. "It seems to be all right. It's just in a very deep sleep."

I told him what had happened, and I showed him the bread crumbs. "I'll bet they've got some sort of sleeping powder in them," he said.

"Poor Annie, I hope she's all right."

I went off to meet Jack. On the way I kept asking myself: "How can I get Annie back? How?" I knew I had to do something. But what?

CHAPTER 8

When I reached the hospital, I called Jack's room to tell him I was there. Then I waited for him in the hospital lobby. He showed up with a big smile on his face.

"Hey, where's my Annie?" he asked.

"She's not here, Jack," I said.

The smile was gone. "What do you mean?" he asked.

I told him what had happened. When I finished, Jack looked very old and very tired. For a minute he didn't say anything.

"It was Weems, all right," he finally said in a whisper. "Weems or one of the people who work for him."

"What will they do with Annie?" I said.

"I don't know," he said. "They'll keep her until the contest is over. I don't know what they'll do after that."

"Jack," I said, "do you think they would hurt her?"

"I — I just hope not," said Jack.

"Maybe the police can help," I said. "They could search Weems's house."

"No," said Jack. "They would have to get

permission from a judge. There's no time for that. There's not much we can do. It looks as if she's gone." There were tears in his eyes.

"I'm sorry, Jack," I said. "It was my fault."

"I don't blame you," he said. "I just wish I could see her again . . . just one more time."

He walked slowly up the hospital stairs. I had never felt so sorry for anyone in my life. I kept thinking I had to do something. But I still didn't know what. I went to a pay phone and called Janie.

"Janie, can you meet me out on Avon Road in about 20 minutes?"

"Sure," she said. "Why?"

I told her I'd explain later.

Avon Road was where Weems's house was. I still didn't have a plan. But maybe one would come to me.

I saw a clock. The time was two-fifteen. The contest started at four. There was still time. I called Jack and told him to meet us at the contest at four.

"Lorna, what are you talking about?" he said. "What are you going to do?"

"It's all right, Jack," I told him. "Please — just be there."

A few minutes later Janie came along. We walked up to Weems's house. It was the biggest house I'd ever seen. There was a big fence all

around it. We walked around the fence until we found what I was looking for. The fence was broken in one spot. It hadn't been fixed yet. We squeezed through.

It was about 200 yards across the grass to the house. We ran all the way. We got to the back entrance of the house. There was an open place where trucks made deliveries. There was also a loading ramp about five feet off the ground. We hopped on the ramp and ran through an open doorway.

And there we were — inside the house. We were in a very large kitchen. Some people were working there. So far, we were lucky. No one had seen us. We saw a door and headed for it.

"Hey!" said a voice. "Hold it!" Someone had seen us. We kept going. We went through one room and then another. Each room was filled with statues, mummy cases, and stone jars. The place was like a museum.

We came to a big, long staircase. We heard voices in the next room. They were coming our

way. I pointed to the staircase. "Let's go!" I said to Janie. We ran up the stairs.

Suddenly a very loud bell went off. It sounded like an alarm. I heard more loud voices downstairs.

We got to the top of the stairs and saw a long hallway. We ran down it. There were two big stone jars at the end of it.

"Quick!" I said. "Let's get in those jars!"

We got in. The bell stopped ringing. We heard footsteps. Someone was coming down a flight of stairs. Then we heard another sound — the sound of a parrot.

"Awwk! Two plus two is four!"

Was that Annie? But Annie wasn't good at math. I couldn't see and I didn't dare lift up my head to look. I heard a voice call, "Mrs. Wade! Mrs. Wade!"

I heard more footsteps. "Yes, Mr. Weems?" came the answer.

"What was that bell for?"

"There are two girls loose in the house."

"Two *girls*?!" said Weems. "Well, *find* them. Don't let them — "

"Awwk! Three plus three is six!" the parrot said.

Was it Annie?

I raised my head slowly and looked out of the jar.

CHAPTER 9

It wasn't Annie. It was a big gray parrot. I ducked right down again.

"Just find those girls," said Weems. "I'm off to the contest at the Coliseum."

"Good luck today, Mr. Weems," said Mrs. Wade.

"I won't need *luck* today," said Weems. "Today I've got the best talking parrot in the world." He turned to the gray parrot. "Aren't you, Cedric?" he said. "We're going to win today, aren't we, boy?"

"Five times seven is thirty-five!" said the parrot.

Big deal. All the bird knew was numbers.

"What about the . . . *other* one?" asked Mrs. Wade.

"Don't worry about the other one," said Weems. He laughed. Then he and Mrs. Wade walked off down the hall.

Janie and I waited until they were gone. Then we climbed out of the jars. We looked around. We saw another flight of stairs.

"Let's go up those stairs," I said. Up we went.

Near the top we heard what we were listening for — bird sounds.

"They're coming from that room," Janie said, pointing.

We went inside. I had never seen so many birds and bird cages in my life. There must have been over a hundred of them. But where was Annie? Was she there at all? We listened. We looked.

"There!" said Janie. "Back there!" She pointed to a large cage in the back. We went to the cage and looked in. Annie lay on the bottom of it. She wasn't moving. She had her little gray blanket around her. All around the bottom of the cage were toasted bread crumbs.

"Annie!" I whispered to her as loudly as I could. "Annie! It's Lorna!"

I poked at her with my finger. She looked up. Her eyes were only half-open.

"You're . . . you're . . . pretty . . ." she said. "You're . . ." She couldn't finish. Her head dropped down again.

I opened the cage. I took all the bread crumbs out of it and stuffed them in my pocket. "Let's get her out of here," I said to Janie.

Just then we heard footsteps behind us. We turned. It was Mrs. Wade. She smiled. "Won't you two come downstairs with me?" she said. She had two guards with her.

The guards came around beside us. They grabbed our arms and led us out of the room.

"What about Annie?" I said. "What are you going to do with Annie?"

"Annie?" she said. "I don't know anything about any Annie. Is she a friend of yours?"

"You know what we mean," said Janie. "The parrot."

Mrs. Wade laughed. "I don't know what you're talking about, dear," she said.

They took us to a small room downstairs. It had a table and some chairs in it. "Sit down, please," Mrs. Wade said.

We sat down. A guard stood at the door.

"How long do you plan to keep us here?" I asked.

"Just a few hours," she said.

I looked at the clock on the wall. It was almost three. The contest started in another hour. It would soon be over. "That's it!" I said to myself. "They'll keep us just until the contest is over."

Time went by. We just sat there while the clock ticked away. Soon it was 3:30.

"Perhaps you girls would like something to eat?" Mrs. Wade asked.

"No, thanks," said Janie. "I'm not hungry."

"We have tomato soup with croutons."

"What are croutons?" I asked.

"They're little toasted bread crumbs," she said. "Would you like to try some?"

I had an idea. "I think I would," I said.

I still had the bread crumbs from Annie's cage. They were in my pocket. Someone came in and set down three bowls of tomato soup. Beside them he set down a bowl of croutons.

The croutons were near Mrs. Wade. I wanted to get to them before she did. I reached for them.

"Don't reach like that!" she snapped. "If you want something — "

"I know," I said. "May I have the croutons, please?"

She passed them over to me. I took a bunch of them. I put them in my soup.

I looked up. Mrs. Wade was looking right at me. She was waiting for me to pass them back to her. I had to get her to look away.

"I wonder what's on TV?" I said. There was a small TV set in the corner.

She got up and went over to turn it on. That was my chance.

CHAPTER 10

Quickly I shoved my hand into my pocket. I pulled out a bunch of the bread crumbs from Annie's cage. I put them on top of the pile of croutons.

Mrs. Wade turned around. She hadn't seen me. "We'll watch some television," she said. "It's too bad the Talking Contest isn't on!" she added, laughing.

I passed her the croutons. She took a handful and put them in her soup.

"The croutons are really good," I said.

She took some more.

Janie gave me a look. She knew what I was doing.

Mrs. Wade called in the guard who was at the door. "Have some soup," she said.

He came in and sat down at the table. He had some tomato soup — with lots of croutons.

It took about 10 minutes for them both to fall asleep. "Let's go," I whispered to Janie. We crept past them. We made it back up the stairs. We got Annie.

"Now where?" we asked each other.

We headed for the kitchen. We figured we'd go out the same way we had come in.

We made it through the kitchen and headed
out the back door. A bread truck was parked at
the back entrance. The door of the truck opened
and the driver got out. He was wearing a
uniform. He looked very much like someone I
knew.

It was Doc!

"Doc!" I called out.

He looked up. "Oh, my gosh!" he said. "Quick!
Get in the back of the truck!"

"Where did you get the truck?" I asked.

"I borrowed it from a friend," he said. He
opened the back door of the truck and we
jumped in.

There, behind 50 loaves of bread, was Captain Jack.

"What are *you two* doing here?!" he said.

"The same thing you are doing here!" I said. "We came for Annie!"

The truck took off. It drove out the back gate. "We're going to the contest," said Jack. "It's not over yet!"

"But — but Annie's asleep!" said Janie.

"She'll be all right," said Jack. "I know Annie. All she needs is a little cup of coffee!"

By the time we got to the contest, it was almost over. Weems's bird, Cedric, was in first place. Weems almost went crazy when we walked in.

Janie and I ran and got some hot coffee. Jack held it up to Annie's beak. She drank a little from the cup.

She looked up. "Hi, Jack!" she said.

A bell rang. A voice announced: "And now — Captain Jack Faraday's parrot, Annie."

"It's time," said Jack. "Here we go, Annie."

He carried Annie up onto a stage. Annie got up on a little wooden stand.

I looked around. There were about 2,000 people in the place and all of them, including Weems, were looking at Annie.

Weems didn't look happy. He was in trouble, and he knew it.

A bell rang again. It was time for Annie to begin.

There was a little microphone in front of her. "Fifteen men on a dead man's chest!" she began. "Ho, ho, ho and a bottle of . . ." Then her head dropped slowly to one side, and she fell asleep again.

A minute went by . . . two minutes . . . three. Wembley Weems began to smile. Captain

Jack looked at the judges. The judges looked back at him.

One of the judges stood up. "Well, if Annie is unable to go on . . . ," he said.

Jack went over to Annie. He put his mouth right next to her head. "HOW'S MY ANNIE?" he said in a very loud voice.

Annie's head jerked up. She woke up in a hurry. "I'm pretty!" she said. "I'm pretty!"

"Yes, you are!" Jack said happily. "How much is two and two?"

"Five!" Annie answered.

Jack laughed. "No, it's not," he said. "It's only *four!*"

"*For* what?" said Annie.

By now everybody was laughing. And Annie was off and talking.

She won the contest. She set a new world's record. She spoke 288 words in 14 different languages. She wouldn't shut up. She talked for six straight hours. And *that* was another new world's record.

By the time she finished, she was wide awake.

But everybody else in the place was asleep.